THE ADVENTURES OF SUPERHERO GIRL

THE ADVENTURES OF SUPERHERO GIRL

WRITTEN AND DRAWN BY

FAITH ERIN HICKS

COLORS BY CRIS PETER

INTRODUCTION BY KURT BUSIEK

DARK HORSE BOOKS

PUBLISHER
MIKE RICHARDSON

EDITOR
RACHEL EDIDIN

ASSISTANT EDITOR
JEMIAH JEFFERSON

DESIGNER
ADAM GRANO

Published by Dark Horse Books
A division of Dark Horse Comics, Inc.
10956 SE Main Street
Milwaukie, OR 97222

DarkHorse.com
SuperheroGirlAdventures.Blogspot.com

First edition: February 2013
ISBN 978-1-61655-084-4

10 9 8 7 6 5 4 3 2

Printed in the United States of America

Mike Richardson, President and Publisher | Neil Hankerson, Executive Vice President | Tom Weddle, Chief Financial Officer | Randy Stradley, Vice President of Publishing | Michael Martens, Vice President of Book Trade Sales | Anita Nelson, Vice President of Business Affairs | Scott Allie, Editor in Chief | Matt Parkinson, Vice President of Marketing | David Scroggy, Vice President of Product Development | Dale LaFountain, Vice President of Information Technology | Darlene Vogel, Senior Director of Print, Design, and Production | Ken Lizzi, General Counsel | Davey Estrada, Editorial Director | Chris Warner, Senior Books Editor | Diana Schutz, Executive Editor | Cary Grazzini, Director of Print and Development | Lia Ribacchi, Art Director | Cara Niece, Director of Scheduling | Tim Wiesch, Director of International Licensing | Mark Bernardi, Director of Digital Publishing

THE ADVENTURES OF (da da DA!) SUPERHERO GIRL

INTRODUCTION

I don't know Faith Erin Hicks, really, aside from the occasional Twitter exchange, or the comment threads on her online strips. And not even that, when I started reading *Superhero Girl*.

No, I came to her work in the old-fashioned way: By looking for good comics for my daughters to read.

Sydney and Katie had gone bananas over Raina Telgemeier's *Smile*, and, no fool I, I went looking for books like it—books that would hook them as hard as comics had hooked me when I was young. I'm a dad; I love comics; and I like to share what I love with my family, so off I went. One of the books I found was Faith's *The War at Ellsmere*, which everyone liked, and that led us to *Superhero Girl*, the online (and later in print) *Friends with Boys,* and the current *Nothing Can Possibly Go Wrong* . . .

And one of the great rewards in looking for cool stuff your daughters will like is that you find new stuff you like, too. It's win-win.

I've liked all of Faith's stuff, and I'm eager for every new page of hers that hits the web or the bookshelves. Her work has charm, energy, emotion, accessibility, and a wonderful sense of humanity. But for all that I'm kind of indiscriminate in liking it—she could adapt the minutes of an Ottawa city council meeting, and I'd want to read it—there's a special place in my heart for *Superhero Girl*.

I'm a superhero fan; I'm a superhero writer; I'm immersed in the genre. Wallowing in it; overthinking it; fat packed with trivia so arcane I can send other superhero obsessives scrambling to *Wikipedia* and Google to find out what the hell I'm talking about. And it's easy, when you're that deep in things, to miss the forest not just for the trees, but for the bark on the trees and the bugs on the bark and the patterns on the wings of the bugs on the . . .

You get the idea.

So I started reading *Superhero Girl* because I'd bought *The War at Ellsmere* and liked it, and my first reaction was, "Cool. A really good superhero parody!"

As time went on, and I read more of it, I realized I was wrong about that.

Not about the "really good" part—*Superhero Girl* is a terrific strip, full of all the great drawing and engaging charm Faith brings to her work. And it's funny. If you've read it before, you know this. If you haven't read it yet, you will. Bear with a Monocle alone would make the strip a winner, but from

5

Spectacle Girl's origin to Superhero Girl's archnemesis Shaun, to Kevin (arrgh, Kevin!), to King Ninja—it's as funny as they come.

It's just not really a parody, is it?

Like I said, steeped in superheroes as I am, it's easy to lose sight of the important stuff, and when you're surrounded by continuity concerns and massive crossovers and often overly grim, overpopulated superhero worlds full of complex and contradictory histories of fictional metals and incomprehensible rules of time travel, it's easy to assume that a funny superhero strip must be a parody of the "real" stuff.

But while Faith is obviously having fun playing with the trappings of the superhero genre, that's not what the strip is really about. Spoofing superheroes isn't the point. She's simply using the genre—genre, as a set of trappings, structures, tropes, whatever gives us a framework in which to tell stories about universal things—to talk about something else.

Superhero Girl is about life. It's about being a younger sister, about being a broke roommate, about needing a job, being underappreciated, getting sick, feeling out of place at parties, being annoyed by people carping when you're doing your best—all wrapped up in the package of being a young superhero in a small-market city where you're pursuing your dreams but don't seem to be getting anywhere.

That's not parody. There may be elements of parody on the surface, but really, that's rich, human storytelling. It's telling the truth through humor, and using the trappings of the superhero genre to universalize it, to turn it into something symbolic, so we can all identify with it, maybe more than we could if SG was a paralegal or a barista or a surgical intern. The superhero stuff is the context, the package, and the humanity and emotion and the humor found in it are the content. The story.

And that's way more about telling a story that connects with readers honestly than a million dimensional wars and fussery about the properties of made-up metals.

The Adventures of Superhero Girl is a superhero story. A funny, human look at how we deal with the craziness of life and dreams and struggle, all dressed up in a cape and a mask and the joy of leaping over tall buildings and biffing some monster clear over the horizon. It's fun. It's charming. It's clever. But above all, it's truthful, funny, and warm.

Or at least, that's the reason why I love *Superhero Girl*. You're going to have your own reason, and it may be completely different from the perspective of a steeped-in-genre, overanalyzing industry professional. But whatever it is, I'm sure you're going to like it, and like me, you're going to hope this is just the first volume of many.

And in case you're wondering: Sydney and Katie haven't read all that much *Superhero Girl*. They come at comics in a different way from their dad—they like graphic novels and collected editions, they're not that into traditionally formatted comic strips, and they've never really latched on to superheroes the way I have. But they like funny comics, they like comics where girls get to be the lead character, and they like comics they can relate to, the ones that are more about people than about cosmic wars. When this book comes out, as a book they can curl up on the couch and spend time with, they'll be all over it.

And that'll be one more thing I get to share with my family.

I hope you'll have as much fun sharing it with yours.

KURT BUSIEK
OCTOBER 2012

SO WHAT'S YOUR SUPER-HERO ORIGIN STORY?

ORIGIN STORY?

YEAH! Y'KNOW, THE CATALYST THAT MADE YOU WANT TO BECOME A SUPERHERO! USUALLY IT'S SOME KINDA TRAGIC OCCURRENCE.

A TRAGEDY THAT **CHANGED** THE WAY YOU SEE THE WORLD ...**FOREVER!**

A TRAGEDY THAT DROVE YOU TO METE OUT *JUSTICE* ON THOSE WHO'D WRONGED YOU!

MY PARENTS ARE DEEAAAAAAD!

SOMETHING LIKE THAT?

GOD, NO.

THEN YOU'RE NOT A REAL SUPERHERO.

FWOOSH

GOOD THING I DID LAUNDRY YESTERDAY...

C'MON C'MON!

SLAM

AW *CRAP!* I FORGOT MY CAPE!

WHATEVER.

IS THAT THE MONSTER YOU'RE FIGHTING?

YEAH.

YOU'RE NOT DOING SUCH A GOOD JOB AT IT.

ARGH, YOU ARE SO ANNOYING!

ANNOYING? ALL I'M DOING IS STANDING HERE.

YOU ARE SUPER ANNOYING. FIRST YOU QUESTION MY VERY SUITABILITY AS A SUPERHERO, AND NOW YOU'VE SHOWN UP TO CRITIQUE MY MONSTER-FIGHTING SKILLS!

IT'S LIKE YOU EXIST JUST TO ANNOY ME!

SLURRP

IT'S LIKE YOU'RE MY--

OH MY GOD.

WHAT?

I KNOW WHO YOU ARE.

HAHA, REALLY? OKAY! WHO AM I?

YOU'RE MY ARCHNEMESIS.

HEY, WHOA. I'M REALLY NOT. HONEST!

25

ZZZZ

HEY.

I'M AWAKE!

YEAH, WELL, YOU'RE LOITERING.

OH, SORRY.

IF YOU'RE GONNA SIT THERE, YOU GOTTA BUY SOMETHING.

OH...UM, I DIDN'T BRING MY WALLET.

THEN YOU CAN'T SIT THERE.

COFFEE

I DID JUST SAVE THIS PLACE FROM GETTING STOMPED ON BY A SPACE MONSTER.

YEAH, THANKS FOR THAT.

GEEZ, FIGHTING THAT SPACE MONSTER WAS...OW. I KNOW SUPERHEROING IS SUPPOSED TO BE ITS OWN REWARD, BUT CAN'T PEOPLE BE A *LITTLE* MORE GRATEFUL..?

MEW.

I KNOW YOU. YOU'RE THAT CAT I GOT OUT OF A TREE A WHILE BACK.

NO NO, YOU CAN'T COME IN! MY ROOMMATE'S ALLERGIC!

OW.

MEW

PURR

PURR

THAT'S BATMAN. HE'S A SUPERHERO LIKE MOMMY.

SHAZBUTT! POW! BAM!

HEY, IS THAT A *CAT*? YOU KNOW WE CAN'T HAVE CATS IN HERE. I'M ALLERGIC.

UM...HE'S, UM, JUST VISITING. I... ER...

I'M TRAINING HIM TO FIGHT CRIME! YEAH! JUST LIKE ME!

MEW

SO HOW COME YOU'LL TEACH SOME CAT THE SECRETS OF CRIME FIGHTING, BUT YOU WON'T TEACH ME?

YOU KNOW I DON'T LIKE MIXING MY HOME LIFE WITH MY WORK.

I DON'T MIND THAT MUCH, BUT IT'S KIND OF ANNOYING TO BE ROOMMATES WITH THE ONLY SUPERHERO IN TOWN WHO WON'T SHARE THE SECRETS OF CRIME FIGHTING.

SORRY, BUT I CAN'T--

OH, DON'T APOLOGIZE. I GET IT.

YOU'RE LIKE COCA-COLA OR KFC: YOU HAVE SECRET INGREDIENTS AND SHARING WOULD BE LIKE REVEALING A TRADE SECRET.

I JUST THINK IT'D BE COOL IF WE COULD BE OUT THERE SAVING THE CITY *TOGETHER*. Y'KNOW, LIKE PARTNERS.

YOU COULD ALWAYS BE MY SIDEKICK.

PLEASE. NO ONE'S THAT DESPERATE.

8:52 AM: HEAD OUT FOR A DAY OF SUPER-HEROING.

9:22 AM: NINJA ATTACK! BUTTS ARE KICKED.

10:29 AM: ASSIST OLDER WOMAN WITH STREET CROSSING.

12:10 PM: LUNCH (CHEESE SANDWICH).

3:33 PM: SAVE ADORABLE CHILD FROM BURNING BUILDING.

5:02 PM: HOME! CAPE IN NEED OF REPAIR.

5:42 PM: REALIZE PERILS OF FORGETTING SUNBLOCK WHILE WEARING A MASK ON A SUNNY DAY.

HEY, ROOMIE, DID YOU--

CAN'T TALK, BUSY. SAVING THE WORLD FROM ALIENS OR ROBOTS OR SOMETHING. THIS GAME IS CONFUSING.

OH MY GOD.

OH MY GODHAHA HAHEEEE

HEEE HAHAHA HAHA

THMP THMP THMP

HAHAH HAA HEE HEE HEH SNF

HEH HEH KOFF SNFF ...AHEM...

FINISHED?

RACCOON GIRL, THAT'S YOUR NEW SUPERHERO NAME.

HEY!

HI!

I HATE SEEING PEOPLE FROM WORK AT THE GROCERY STORE.

beep
Beep boop

ATM

BANK ACCOUNT BALANCE: $7.52

GI_ US MORE _ONEY!

YOU'RE **BROKE?**

KINDA, YEAH.

LAST YEAR I GOT A GRANT FROM THE GOVERNMENT WHICH LET ME DO MY SUPERHEROING FULL TIME...

...BUT NOW I'VE KINDA USED UP THAT MONEY.

GUESS I GOTTA GET A JOB THAT ACTUALLY PAYS...

...AND PUT THE SUPERHERO THING ON HOLD FOR A BIT.

SO, KNOW OF ANY EMPLOYERS NEEDING PEOPLE?

I MIGHT. DEPENDS ON WHAT KIND OF SKILLS YOU HAVE.

UM...I CAN WEAR A CAPE...WHICH IS HARDER THAN IT LOOKS...UMM...I CAN LIFT HEAVY OBJECTS...

OH, AND I CAN LEAP OVER ANY BUILDING SHORTER THAN ELEVEN STORIES.

THINK I COULD GET HIRED ANYWHERE?

YEP, YOU'VE GOT THE EXACT QUALIFICATIONS THEY'RE LOOKING FOR AT TIM HORTONS.

33

HI!

THIS IS KINDA FUN!

I DON'T GO ON JOB INTERVIEWS VERY OFTEN.

ARE YOU INTERVIEWING FOR THE JOB TOO?

ER, YES.

UM, YOU HAVE--

OH, DOES MY HAIR LOOK WEIRD? I USED MY ROOMMATE'S FLAT IRON.

NO, IT'S--

CRAP, IS THERE SOMETHING ON MY FACE?

YEAH, YOU COULD SAY THAT...

AARRGHA I FORGOT TO TAKE OFF MY MASK AGAIN

JUST TAKE IT OFF NOW! THE INTERVIEW HASN'T STARTED YET.

...BUT YOU'LL KNOW MY SECRET IDENTITY!

OH MY GOD, WHY AM I SO BAD AT THIS SUPERHERO THING?

OH, C'MON, YOU'RE NOT BAD AT ALL!

REMEMBER WHEN YOU SAVED THE CITY FROM THAT SPACE MONSTER? THAT WAS REALLY COOL.

YEAH, I GUESS.

CRASH!

HAH! FOUND YOU!

YOU CAN NEVER ESCAPE THE WRATH OF KING NINJA, SUPER-HERO GIRL!

YOU MUST--

DUDE, C'MON! I'M IN THE MIDDLE OF A JOB INTERVIEW! I'M TRYING TO FIND EMPLOYMENT!

REALLY? YOU'RE HAVING MONEY ISSUES?

KINDA.

I DON'T GET PAID A SALARY FOR THE SUPERHERO THING. IT'S VOLUNTARY.

WOW. ...HUH. OH HEY, YOU KNOW WHAT DOES PAY?

CRIME!! MUAHAHA!

I'M REALLY SORRY ABOUT ALL THIS.

SO NOT ONLY DID KING NINJA GET THE JOB, BUT HE ENDED UP BEING SO GOOD AT IT THAT HE GAVE UP HIS LIFE OF CRIME TO WORK IN FINANCE?

YEAH.

GOOD FOR HIM!

SHUT UP.

BRRRIINNG

PUT IT BACK.

BEING A SUPERHERO ISN'T SO TOUGH ONCE YOU GET THE LOCAL CRIMINAL ELEMENT TRAINED.

HEY, DID YOU HEAR THE NEWS?

WHAT NEWS?

KEVIN'S IN TOWN!

KEVIN?? THAT'S SO COOL! I *LOVE* HIM!

I HEARD KEVIN FLEW IN THIS MORNING.

YEAH, ME TOO. I LOVE THAT GUY. HE'S AMAZING.

HI, KEVIN.

HI, SIS! HOW'D YOU FIND OUT I WAS IN TOWN?

MOM'S TOLD ME ABOUT YOUR SITUATION, SIS, AND THE PROBLEM'S OBVIOUS.

I DON'T LOOK LIKE A SUPERHERO.

EXACTLY. YOU DON'T LOOK LIKE A SUPER-HERO.

UGH. SO I'M NOT SOME GIANT MUSCLEY GUY WITH A CORPORATE LOGO ON MY CHEST, SO WHAT? WHAT DOES THAT *MATTER?*

YOU SHOULDN'T *NEED* THAT STUFF TO BE A SUPERHERO!

YOU'RE RIGHT. YOU SHOULDN'T NEED TO LOOK A CERTAIN WAY.

BOTH YOU AND I KNOW THAT CLOTHES AND MUSCLES DO NOT MAKE A COMPETENT SUPERHERO. IT *DOESN'T* MATTER.

BUT IT MATTERS TO *THEM*.

SO THINK ABOUT WHAT I'VE SAID, SIS.

IT DOESN'T HURT TO PLAY THE GAME AND HAVE A MORE ...CONVENTIONAL SUPER- HERO IDENTITY.

YEAH, I'M NOT GOING TO DO THAT.

OKAY, WELL, I TRIED.

I'LL TELL MOM YOU'RE CONTENT TO LIVE LIFE IN THE SUPERHERO MARGINS.

KEVIN AWESOME

HELLO, MY ADORING PUBLIC!

EEEEE KEVIN!

HEY, IS THAT KEVIN?

YES.

. . .

MAN, I CAN'T STAND THAT GUY. HE BUGS ME.

REALLY?

GOOD THING I BROUGHT MY SHRINK-RAY GUN.

FWIP

TO BE CONTINUED! ...OR NOT. YA DON'T KNOW, DO YA!

44

WHOA WHOA WHOA!

YOU *CANNOT* SHRINK RAY KEVIN!

WHY NOT? HE'S ANNOYING. WOULDN'T HE BE LESS ANNOYING IF HE WERE TINY?

HAHAHAHA

YOU'RE SO WIDDLE!

YES YOU ARE!

GGGNNNGH!

YOU'RE IMAGINING HIM TINY, AREN'T YOU?

NNNOO.

45

KEVIN MAY BE ANNOYING, BUT I CAN'T LET YOU SHRINK RAY HIM. I'M A SUPERHERO. IT'S MY JOB TO PROTECT PEOPLE.

EVEN WHEN THEY *ARE* COMPLETELY OBNOXIOUS.

YOU'RE SURE ABOUT THAT?

YEP!

WHAT'S YOUR DEAL WITH KEVIN ANYWAY?

YOU *CAN'T* BE A SUPER-VILLAIN.

FWIP

I CAN'T BE A SUPERVILLAIN? WHY CAN'T I?

C'MON, DUDE. YOU DON'T LOOK *ANYTHING* LIKE A SUPERVILLAIN.

THAT'S PRETTY IRONIC, COMING FROM YOU.

I MEAN, WHAT'S YOUR SUPERVILLAIN NAME? THE INCREDIBLE SHRINKING HIPSTER?

WHAT ARE YOU WRITING?

WRITING MY NEW YEAR'S RESOLUTIONS!

I RESOLVE TO BE A BETTER SUPERHERO.

I WILL FIGHT CRIME TO THE BEST OF MY ABILITIES AND MAKE THE WORLD A BETTER PLACE.

TO BE A BEACON OF HOPE TO THOSE IN DESPAIR.

I RESOLVE THAT IF THERE IS EVEN ONE CITIZEN COWERING IN FEAR BEFORE THE SPECTRE OF CRIME, I WILL BE THE ONE TO PUNCH THAT SPECTRE IN THE FACE!

...IF IT HAS A FACE. IF NOT, I'LL PUNCH IT WHEREVER.

ALSO, I RESOLVE TO GET A PROPER JOB SO I CAN PAY MY HALF OF THE RENT.

YEAH, THIS CITIZEN WOULD APPRECIATE THAT.

STONE WINCHESTER HERE TO BRING YOU THIS SPECIAL REPORT ABOUT A CRIME WAVE SWEEPING OUR FAIR CITY.

DOZENS OF LOCAL GROCERIES WERE BURGLED LAST NIGHT, THE SAME SHADOWY FIGURE SHOWING UP ON MULTIPLE SECURITY CAMERAS. THE CRIME? **MARSHMALLOW THEFT**. VICTIMS OF THE CRIME SPEAK OUT:

I...I CAME INTO THE STORE TO GET MARSHMALLOWS FOR MY MORNING CUP OF HOT CHOCOLATE...

AND... THEY TOLD ME ALL THE MARSH-MALLOWS HAD BEEN... STOLEN.

FWIP

AND WHO IS THE CULPRIT BEHIND THIS APPALLING CRIME WAVE? REPORTS INDICATE A NEW SUPERVILLAIN MAY BE ON THE LOOSE. HE IS KNOWN AS--

--THE MARSH-MALLOW MENACE.

IT'S SO LAME WHAT PASSES FOR VILLAINY IN THIS CITY.

NEXT UP: SOME RANDOM GUY IS TOTALLY APPALLED BY THE CRIME!

I AM **SHOCKED**! SOCIETY **CRUMBLES** AROUND US!

SLAM

YOU WOULDN'T BELIEVE WHERE I'VE BEEN.

YOU WERE FIGHTING MARSH-MALLOW DUDE! IT WAS ON TV. YOU LOOKED GOOD!

I *DID NOT* LOOK GOOD! IT WAS EMBARRASSING!

HE THREW *MARSHMALLOWS* AT ME!

WHY ARE THE SUPERVILLAINS IN THIS CITY SO *LAME*? HOW DO I GET TAKEN SERIOUSLY AS A SUPERHERO IF *THESE* ARE THE KIND OF VILLAINS I'M FIGHTING?

MY LIFE SUCKS SO MUCH. *SO. MUCH.*

ARRGGHH

Y'KNOW, MAYBE YOU COULD JUST BE HAPPY YOU DON'T LIVE IN A CITY THAT'S OVERRUN WITH CRIME.

THAT WOULD BE *AWESOME*! I *WISH* THIS CITY WAS OVERRUN WITH CRIME.

SO? THE PARTY IS FUN, RIGHT?

YEAH! IT'S NICE TO HANG OUT WITH PEOPLE WHO AREN'T SUPER-VILLAINS.

I'M GOING TO TALK TO THAT GUY.

GOOD FOR YOU!

HI!

HI!

I GOTTA GO!

...OH.

WHAT HAPPENED?

I'VE FORGOTTEN HOW TO TALK TO PEOPLE I DON'T NEED TO PUNCH.

OKAY! DON'T GET DISCOURAGED! SO YOU'RE A LITTLE OUT OF PRACTICE WITH THE SMALL TALK! NO BIG DEAL.

IF WE TALK TO SOMEONE TOGETHER, MAYBE YOU'LL FEEL MORE COMFORTABLE.

YAY!

HEY, THAT GUY LOOKS COOL. LET'S TALK TO HIM.

NO. WE ARE NOT TALKING TO HIM.

WHY NOT? HE SEEMS REALLY NICE.

WE ARE NOT TALKING TO HIM BECAUSE HE IS CLEARLY A SUPERVILLAIN!

WHAT? NO, HE'S NOT. HE JUST DRESSES FANCY.

HELLO!

HI! ENJOYING THE PARTY?

VERY MUCH SO. I AM NEW TO THIS CITY, HERE TO SEEK MY FORTUNE. SO FAR I'VE MET SOME *VERY* NICE PEOPLE.

THAT'S GREAT! I'M SO HAPPY FOR YOU!

RIGHT NOW I AM LOOKING HARD FOR SPECIAL PEOPLE TO BE A PART OF MY ... ORGANIZATION. THERE WILL BE SOME LIGHT VILLAINY, POSSIBLE ATTEMPTS AT WORLD DOMINATION DOWN THE ROAD. DOES THAT SOUND INTERESTING?

OOH, IT DOES! I WOULD LOVE TO WORK FOR YOU!

I HAVE THIS SUPERPOWER. IT MAKES EVERYONE THINK THAT I AM AWESOME.

YOU *ARE*. YOU ARE *TOTALLY* AWESOME.

THEY SAY WITH GREAT POWER COMES GREAT RESPONSIBILITY, BUT...EH!

I WOULD RATHER RULE THE WORLD AND HAVE A SOLID-GOLD TOILET, YOU KNOW?

I *DO* KNOW! SOMEONE AS AWESOME AS YOU *SHOULD* RULE THE WORLD!

Panel 1: THIS IS *BAD*.

Panel 2: EVERYONE AT THIS PARTY HAS BEEN SEDUCED BY A SUPERVILLAIN WHO HAS THE POWER TO MAKE PEOPLE THINK HE'S AWESOME. EVEN THOUGH HE'S A *SUPERVILLAIN*!

Panel 3: THAT JERK HAS TURNED FREE-WILLED PEOPLE INTO MINDLESS ZOMBIES!

Panel 4: ONLY I, THE ORDINARY ROOM-MATE OF A LOCAL SUPERHERO, SEEM IMMUNE TO HIS CHARMS!

Panel 5: THE *IRONY*! IF ONLY MY CRIME-FIGHTING ROOMMATE HAD TRAINED ME IN THE MYSTIC ARTS OF SUPERHEROING...

...THEN I, *POSSIBLY THE ONLY PERSON ABLE TO DEFEAT THIS VILLAIN*, COULD SAVE THE DAY!

Panel 6: BUT I HAVE NO SUPERPOWERS OF MY OWN.

HOW CAN I, AN ORDINARY HUMAN, HOPE TO WIN THIS FIGHT?

Panel 7: I MUST USE MY WITS TO DEFEAT HIM!

Panel 8: UM, HEY!... HAVING FUN TONIGHT?

SILENCE, INTERLOPER! I'M *NARRATING*!

I HAVE TO MAKE MY SUPERHERO ROOMMATE SEE THAT THE GUY SHE THINKS IS AWESOME IS ACTUALLY A JERK SUPER-VILLAIN. BUT *HOW*??

SO I AM THINKING AFTER I TAKE OVER THE WORLD, I COULD HAVE MANY STATUES BUILT THAT LOOK LIKE ME.

THAT IS SUCH A GREAT IDEA!

VEGGIE DIP ATTACK!

SP*L*UT

MAYBE IF YOU MADE HIM LOOK ...NOT AWESOME?

GOOD IDEA!

TWIP

JUMP

HOLY *CRAP!* THIS GUY'S A *SUPER-VILLAIN!*

THIS RANCH DRESSING SURE IS GOOD WITH CARROTS.

POW!!

WSST

EXCUSE ME. I HAVE AN ASS TO KICK.

YAY!

THIS WEEKEND KIND OF FELT LIKE ONE HUGE LIFE LESSON ABOUT BEING A SUPER-HERO.

YOU THINK?

YEAH.

IT REALLY DROVE HOME THE IMPORTANCE OF BALANCE IN A SUPER-HERO'S LIFE. YOU CAN'T BE A SUPERHERO ALL THE TIME, AND YOU SHOULDN'T WANT TO BE.

IT'S REALLY IMPORTANT TO PUT ASIDE THE CAPE AND THE MASK SOMETIMES AND JUST BE ORDINARY. ORDINARY'S IMPORTANT IN A SUPER-HEROIC LIFE.

BUT IT'S TOUGH TO BALANCE, BECAUSE ONE LIFE KEEPS INFRINGING ON THE OTHER. LIKE WHEN YOU GO TO A PARTY AND IT TURNS OUT THE GUY YOU'RE TALKING TO IS A SUPERVILLAIN, SO YOU HAVE TO DEFEAT HIM.

WELL, I'M GLAD WHAT HAPPENED MADE YOU REALIZE THAT.

YEAH.

IT REALLY MAKES YOU THINK.

IT MAKES ME THINK I'M NEVER LETTING MY ROOM-MATE DRAG ME TO PARTIES WHERE A LIFE LESSON IS WAITING TO PUNCH ME IN THE FACE.

YOU WON'T LEARN ANYTHING AT THE NEXT PARTY, I PROMISE.

HI! I'M SPECTACLE.

ER... HELLO.

YOU'RE SUPERHERO GIRL, RIGHT?

WELL, THAT'S WHAT EVERYONE CALLS ME, BUT IT'S NOT REALLY MY NAME.

I'M A REALLY BIG FAN OF YOUR WORK. I THINK WHAT YOU DO IS FANTASTIC.

I THINK IT'S SO AMAZING HOW EVERY DAY YOU GO OUT AND FIGHT CRIME ON YOUR OWN TERMS.

YOU'RE A BIG INSPIRATION TO ME.

ANYWAY, I GOTTA GO. JUST WANTED TO SAY HI.

WHAT JUST HAPPENED?

DOINK

TRIP

OH CRAP.

WAAGGHH

CRACK

WHAT I REALLY NEED IS IDIOT-PROOF SUPERPOWERS.

MOMMY! THAT SUPERHERO SUCKS!

HUSH, CHILD.

HEY ROOMIE, I'VE DECIDED SINCE YOU HELPED ME DEFEAT THAT LAST SUPERVILLAIN, I'M GOING TO LET YOU IN ON THE SECRETS OF SUPER-HEROING.

THAT'S GREAT! BUT I CAN'T TONIGHT. I'M GOING OUT.

I HAVE A DATE WITH A GUY I MET AT THAT PARTY. HE'S THE ONE WHO SUGGESTED I HIT THAT SUPERVILLAIN WITH THE VEGGIE DIP.

...OH.

WISH ME LUCK!

YEAH... HAVE A GOOD TIME.

FWIP

KITTY, I WILL TEACH YOU THE SECRETS OF SUPERHEROING AND TOGETHER WE WILL DEFEAT CRIME.

KITTY, DON'T LEAVE MEEEE NNNNOOOOO.

POOP.

I HAD A REALLY GREAT NIGHT! WHAT'D YOU DO WHILE I WAS OUT?

I DISCOVERED I DESPERATELY NEED A HOBBY.

POLICE BLOTTER
NO CRIME TO REPORT!
TAKE THE NIGHT OFF, EVERYBODY!

POLICE BLOTTER
SERIOUSLY, NO CRIME TO REPORT AT ALL!

I HAVE A LOT OF SPARE TIME RIGHT NOW. ALL THE LOCAL SUPERVILLAINS SEEM TO BE... WELL, *BETWEEN* WORLD DOMINATION PLANS--

--AND REGULAR CRIME JUST ISN'T AS TIME CONSUMING AS SUPERVILLAIN CRIME.

AND MY ROOMMATE HAS A NEW BOYFRIEND--I'M *TOTALLY* HAPPY FOR HER, BUUUUT--

UM... WELL, MY SISTER KNITS...

YEAH! SHE MAKES *GREAT* SWEATERS.

OOH, KNITTING. THAT'S A START.

WELL, YOU KNOW. THREE'S A CROWD AND ALL THAT. SO NOT HANGING OUT WITH HER MUCH, LATELY.

ANYWAY, I'VE DECIDED I REALLY NEED A HOBBY. SOMETHING TO FILL MY TIME WHILE THE SUPERHERO THING IS SLOW. I'VE NEVER REALLY HAD A HOBBY BEFORE 'CAUSE MY JOB IS USUALLY SO TIME CONSUMING.

SO! ANYONE WANT TO SUGGEST SOMETHING HOBBY-ISH TO PICK UP? SOMETHING COOL!

SUPERHERO GIRL IN

ADVENTURES IN KNITTING

CRAP. I TOTALLY DID IT WRONG *AGAIN!*

WELL, WASN'T THAT THRILLING? SEE YOU NEXT WEEK, FOLKS!

SNERK

BAHAHAHAHA

HA HAHA HA HA
HA HA
HA HAHA HAHAHA
HA HA
HA HAHA

WHAP WHAP

THANKS FOR THE HELP ROUNDING UP THESE VILLAINS, SUPERHERO GIRL! SUPERVILLAINS ARE A LOT EASIER TO CATCH WHEN THEY'RE HELPLESS WITH LAUGHTER.

YEAH, IT WAS ALL PART OF MY BRILLIANT PLAN.

HAHAHA IT LOOKS LIKE A BLIND MONKEY KNITTED THAT SWEATER!

OHHH MY *GOD* WHAT *IS* THAT I DON'T EVEN *KNOW!*

HILARIOUS

HAAAHA HAHA

BEEP BEEP BEEP BEEP

NNOO TOO EARLY...

7:00

YAWN

HOLY BAD HAIR DAY. I CAN'T FIGHT CRIME LOOKING LIKE THIS.

BRUSH BRUSH

SPROING!

THERE, PROBLEM SOLVED.

TODAY IS A HOOD-UP DAY.

HAHAHA! I LOOK KINDA EVIL! LIKE A SITH LORD!

LUUUKE I AM YOUR FAAATHERR.

GASP!

TONIGHT AT 11! SUPERHERO GIRL TURNS EVIL AND WE HAVE THE FILM TO PROVE IT!

WHAT IS WRONG WITH THIS CITY?

RIIING

. . .

I WAS HAVING A BAD HAIR DAY AND I WORE A HOODIE WITH THE HOOD UP. I KNOW, IT TOTALLY MAKES ME LOOK ALL SITH LORD--

FWIP

HELLO?

HI, MOM!

I WASN'T EXPECTING --WHAT?

NO, I *HAVEN'T* TURNED *EVIL!* WHO TOLD YOU *THAT*??

YOU SAW IT ON TV?

WELL, IT'S *NOT* TRUE! IT'S ALL A MISUNDERSTANDING.

KABOOM

WORD OF YOUR CONVERSION TO SUPERVILLAINY HAS REACHED ME, SUPERHERO GIRL! THOUGH IT PAINS ME TO DO SO, IT IS NOW MY DUTY TO DEFEAT YOU.

MOM, I GOTTA GO. A MISUNDERSTANDING JUST BLEW A HOLE IN MY DAMAGE DEPOSIT.

NOW THAT YOU'RE EVIL, SHOULDN'T YOU UPGRADE TO SOME KIND OF UNDERGROUND LAIR?

71

YOU BLEW UP MY HOUSE! THIS IS *NOT COOL!*

AND THE TV'S SMASHED! MY ROOMMATE'S GOING TO KILL ME.

YOU'VE GOT BIGGER PROBLEMS THAN A SMASHED TV, SUPER-HERO GIRL!

OR SHOULD I SAY, SUPER*VILLAIN* GIRL?

NO! NO SUPER-VILLAIN GIRL! THIS IS ALL A MISTAKE!

I CAN'T TAKE THAT RISK. IF YOU'VE TURNED EVIL, YOU'RE A THREAT.

THIS IS GOING TO HURT ME MORE THAN IT'LL HURT YOU!

FWAP

FLAIL FLAIL

ehhnn

WHEN DID FREAKISHLY LONG ARMS BECOME YOUR SUPERPOWER?

JUST NOW, APPARENTLY.

EEP.

SERIOUSLY--

I'M NOT--

--EVIL!

THIS IS WHY I HAVE TO DEFEAT YOU!

NADIAN CHRON

SUPERHERO GIRL KIDNAPS PM, DEMANDS BANNING OF HOCKEY, TIM HORTON'S COFF

STATE OF EMERGE DECLARED AS RIOTS, COFFEE HOARDING REPORTED

I JUST WORE A HOODIE WITH THE HOOD UP!

I DON'T THINK YOU'RE EVIL BECAUSE OF THAT! I'M NOT STUPID!

HOW CAN A PHOTOGRAPH GO "HAHAHAHA"?

THERE'RE MORE PICTURES INSIDE. CHECK OUT YOUR EVIL HAIRDO!

THIS IS *NOT ME* KIDNAPPING THE PRIME MINISTER.

IT'S NOT?

NO!!!

BUT SHE LOOKS EXACTLY LIKE YOU.

SHE DOES *NOT!*

SHE HAS AN UPSIDE-DOWN HEART ON HER CHEST. I WEAR A STAR.

OH, GOSH.

UM, YEAH. *HELLO!*

OH, MY GOSH. I CAN'T BELIEVE...

OH, HEY, DON'T BEAT YOURSELF UP. SHE DOES LOOK PRETTY SIMILAR TO ME. ANYONE COULD'VE MADE THAT MISTAKE--

THIS IS AWESOME!

NOW WE GET TO TEAM UP TO DEFEAT YOUR EVIL DOPPELGANGER!!

WHAT.

C'MON, C'MON!

WAIT, YOU'RE NOT EVEN SORRY A LITTLE? DO YOU SEE THE SMOKING HOLE WHERE MY ROOF USED TO BE?

SUPERVILLAIN GIRL WAS SPOTTED AROUND HERE A FEW DAYS AGO, SO MAYBE SHE'LL TURN UP.

SO WHY'D YOU BECOME A SUPERHERO?

OH, IT WAS SOMETHING I'D ALWAYS WANTED TO DO, EVER SINCE I WAS A KID.

REALLY? YOU DON'T HAVE SOME TRAGEDY IN YOUR PAST--

WHAT?? NO!

SOMETIMES PEOPLE JUST *WANT* TO BE SUPERHEROES! IT'S NOT BECAUSE OUR PARENTS WERE MURDERED OR WE'RE SOME RICH SOCIALITE WITH TOO MUCH TIME ON OUR HANDS! SOME OF US JUST *WANT* TO BE SUPERHEROES! THAT'S IT!

WHAT ABOUT YOU? WHY'D YOU BECOME A SUPERHERO?

I'M A RICH SOCIALITE WITH TOO MUCH TIME ON MY HANDS.

OF COURSE YOU ARE.

SO YOU DO THE SUPER-HEROING BY NIGHT AND YOUR DAY JOB IS...SOCIALITE?

SOMETIMES! I DO GET INVITED TO A LOT OF PARTIES. BUT MOSTLY I MODEL. IT PAYS THE BILLS.

MODELLING'S REALLY... WELL, IT'S ALL SO SUPERFICIAL.

I'VE ALWAYS WANTED TO DO SOMETHING THAT GIVES BACK TO MY COMMUNITY.

AND THEN--WELL, YOU KNOW HOW IT IS--I GET HIT BY A SUPER-SECRET GOVERNMENT SPACE RAY AND SUDDENLY I CAN FLY AND PUNCH THINGS REALLY WELL.

I DECIDED TO FIGHT CRIME WITH MY NEW SUPERPOWERS.

BUT KEEPING MY CIVILIAN IDENTITY A SECRET WAS GOING TO BE A PROBLEM, SINCE I'M IN A LOT OF MAGAZINES AND TV COMMERCIALS.

SO I CAME UP WITH A SOLUTION...

SEE? GLASSES OFF AND YOU CAN'T EVEN TELL IT'S ME!

OH MY GOD YOU'RE RIGHT YOU DO LOOK COMPLETELY DIFFERENT!

YEAH! IT'S KIND OF AMAZING HOW WELL IT WORKS.

YES. TRULY, TRULY AMAZING.

UM, ARE YOU MAD AT ME?

NNOOO, I'M SORRY. I'M JUST FRUSTRATED.

SOME CRAZY SUPERVILLAIN GIRL IS IMPERSONATING ME, AND WE DON'T HAVE ANY IDEA WHERE SHE IS--

HELLO!

AAHHH! SUPERVILLAIN GIRL!

I LIKE KITTENS.

OOF!

CATCH!

MY CAT'S NAME IS STANLEYYY...

DID THE PRIME MINISTER JUST SAY HIS CAT'S NAME IS STANLEY?

YES! AND SOMETIME IN THE FUTURE THAT VERY CAT WILL INVENT AN AFFORDABLE TIME MACHINE. HE'S VERY SMART.

I CAN'T BELIEVE I BECAME A **SUPERVILLAIN** TEN YEARS IN THE FUTURE JUST BECAUSE I HAD A CRAPPY WEEK!

BELIEVE IT, YOUNGER ME. I'M SICK OF ALL THE UNGRATEFUL CITIZENS WHOSE BUTTS I JUST SAVED, OF BEING TOLD I SUCK JUST BECAUSE I DON'T HAVE FLASHY SUPERPOWERS OR A CORPORATE SPONSOR. I'M SICK OF NEVER GETTING WHAT *I* WANT.

ENOUGH OF THIS CRAPPY SUPERHERO LIFE! I WANT TO BE **RICH** AND **POWERFUL**, LIKE A SUPERVILLAIN!!

SINCE THE EASIEST WAY TO GET RICH IS TO STEAL A BUNCH OF DOUGH--

--I DECIDED TO TIME TRAVEL TO THE PAST WHEN I WAS A CRAPPY SUPERHERO WHO HAD NO CHANCE OF STOPPING AN OLDER, MORE AWESOME VERSION OF HERSELF.

SO LET'S FIGHT.

YOU'LL LOSE BECAUSE I'VE GOT TEN YEARS' EXPERIENCE ON YOU, AND I'LL STEAL ALL THE GOLD AND JEWELS THIS TIME PERIOD HAS ON HAND, AND TAKE THEM BACK WITH ME.

I CAN'T BELIEVE WHAT A BUTTHEAD I AM IN THE FUTURE.

YEAH, WELL, THAT'S HOW IT IS: YOU TURN THIRTY AND IT'S TIME FOR MAMA TO GET *PAID*.

I FEEL SORRY FOR YOU, SUPERVILLAIN GIRL. YOU'VE FORGOTTEN WHY YOU BECAME A SUPER-HERO IN THE FIRST PLACE.

I DON'T CARE ABOUT THAT ANY-MORE.

BECAUSE BEING A SUPERHERO IS THE THING WE LOVE BEST IN THE WORLD.

SUCKER PUNCH THROUGH TIME & SPACE

BINK

A PART OF YOU STILL MUST! WHY ELSE WOULD YOU COME TO THE PAST TO CONFRONT YOUR YOUNGER SELF?

YOU'RE HERE TO WARN ME TO NEVER LOSE SIGHT OF WHY I BECAME A SUPERHERO!

WHY'D I EVEN BECOME ONE?

I CAN'T REMEMBER ANYMORE!

WHA-WHAT HAVE I DOOONNE??

SHHH, COME HERE--

WELL, I SURE HOPE THAT DOESN'T COME BACK TO HAUNT ME.

EH, IT'S TIME TRAVEL, WHAT COULD POSSIBLY GO WRONG?

IT'S NOT EVERY DAY YOU GET TO DEFEAT AN EVIL FUTURE VERSION OF YOURSELF. I'D SAY YOU'VE JOINED THE RANKS OF THE TRULY ELITE.

YEAH, WELL, I'M JUST HAPPY IT'S OVER.

IS IT REALLY OVER, THOUGH? SUPPOSEDLY YOU'LL BECOME A SUPERVILLAIN SOME TIME IN THE FUTURE.

NO, I WON'T.

I'LL NEVER ALLOW MYSELF TO BECOME SUPERVILLAIN GIRL.

I KNOW WHY I'M A SUPER-HERO. AND I KNOW THAT IF SUPERHEROING EVER BECOMES A BURDEN, I'LL STOP DOING IT.

GLAD TO HEAR IT. WANT TO HELP ME GET THE PRIME MINISTER HOME?

SURE.

HE SEEMS TO BE ATTRACTING A LOT OF CATS.

WEIRD.

KITTIEEES!

AND THEN STARLADY PUNCHED THE EVIL SUPEREVIL MAN RIGHT IN HIS STOOPID FACE--

WHOOoSH

HAHAHA! I GOT YOUR DUMB DOLL AND YOU GOTTA COME UP HERE TO GET IT! BUT YOU CAN'T 'CAUSE YOU CAN'T FLY!

I HATE YOU, KEVIN! I'M TELLING! MOOOM!

KEVIN, WHY ARE YOU TEASING YOUR LITTLE SISTER? YOU KNOW SHE DOESN'T HAVE FLYING SUPERPOWERS LIKE YOU.

SNIFF

NOW APOLOGIZE.

NYAAH

POW
BZAP
WHAMM POKE
AHHH

THOSE PARENTING BOOKS DID NOT PREPARE ME FOR THIS.

BZAP!
bop bop bop

OW! NO FAIR USING HEAT VISION! MOM!

HEY SIS! WORKING HARD?

YES, KEVIN. THERE'S A TEST TOMORROW. GOTTA STUDY.

I THINK IT'S SO COMMENDABLE THAT YOU WORK HARD AT YOUR EDUCATION. I ADMIRE THAT.

EEEK! THE ROBOT LIBRARIAN HAS GONE CRAZY! SOMEBODY STOP IT!

WHOOPS, I THINK THAT'S FOR ME!

POW KRAK WHAMM

FZZT

YEAH, IT'S SO COMMENDABLE YOU STUDY SO HARD. I'VE GOT SUPER MEMORY POWERS SO TESTS ARE A SNAP FOR ME, BUT NOT FOR YOU! BUT HERE YOU ARE, WO...

blurrghh BLAAHHGG

Ick

Sploorch

THE BLOB FAMILY! THIS IS GOING TO BE...*GROSS.*

WHAP

BLISSH

WHAP

OOF

SPLUT

EWW!

GLURP

bloop

blurg

NEVER FEAR, KEVIN'S HERE!

WAIT, I CAN HANDLE--

Ick

blop

blek Blurg

KER-POW!

HAH *HAH!* LOOK AT THEM RUN!

HEY, I HAD IT UNDER CONTROL.

SURE YOU DID. NOW WAVE!

HAH HA, WE BEAT THAT BLOB FAMILY BUT GOOD! AND WHO KNOWS WHAT EVIL WE WILL DEFEAT IN THE NEXT FEW MONTHS!

YEAH, I NEED TO TALK TO YOU ABOUT THAT.

UM, I'VE DECIDED I WANT TO GO TO UNIVERSITY OUT EAST...

SO, UM, I'M GOING TO START SUPERHEROING THERE INSTEAD.

I KNOW WE'VE BEEN WORKING TOGETHER FOR A WHILE, BUT ...WELL...

I WANT TO DO MY OWN THING.

HAHAH, OF COURSE! YOU HAVE TO FIND YOUR OWN SUPERHERO PATH.

I COMPLETELY UNDERSTAND.

hop

I THOUGHT WE WERE A TEAM...

YE OLDE
UNIVERSITY
EST. 1902
(YES, THIS IS STILL A FLASHBACK)

THP. THP. THP. THP. THP

OUR NINJA KING HAS SENT US IN SEARCH OF MORE BOOZE, WHICH WE WILL NOW STEAL FROM THAT UNATTENDED COOLER--

FWOOSH

NO, YA WON'T!

POW WHAM KRAK

WE WERE ATTACKED ON OUR MISSION, MY LIEGE! A SUPERHERO GIRL CAME OUT OF NOWHERE AND BEAT THE CRAP OUT OF US.

SO, SOME FRESHMAN DO-GOODER THINKS SHE CAN GET IN THE WAY OF *MY* EVIL PLOTS? WE'LL SEE ABOUT THAT.

SOON YOU WILL KNOW MY WRATH, SUPERHERO GIRL! OR MY NAME ISN'T... *KING NINJA!*

DUDE, YOUR NAME IS TREVOR.

SHUT UP! WHY YOU ALWAYS GOTTA RUIN MY SUPER-VILLAIN MOMENT, LARRY?

CLAREMONT UNIVERSITY STRIVES FOR A POLICY OF TOLERANCE. HOWEVER, OCCASIONALLY WE HAVE A STUDENT WITH VERY ...*PARTICULAR* NEEDS.

AND SOMETIMES WE FIND OURSELVES *UNABLE* TO MEET THAT STUDENT'S NEEDS...

WE FEEL THAT AS A SCHOOL, WE ARE NOT EQUIPPED TO DEAL WITH THE NINJA ATTACKS.

SNEAK NINJA ATTACK!

LEAP!

POW

THAT'S OKAY! *I'M* EQUIPPED TO DEAL WITH THEM.

YES, BUT OUR INSURANCE PREMIUMS AREN'T.

MOM SAID YOU GOT KICKED OUT OF SCHOOL FOR SUPERHEROING!

I REALLY HOPE YOU DIDN'T FLY ALL THE WAY HERE TO POINT THAT OUT.

WHATEVER, IT'S FINE. I THINK I NEED A BREAK FROM SCHOOL NOW ANYWAY.

I WANT TO BE A SUPER-HERO FULL TIME.

THAT'S GREAT!

YOU'LL COME HOME AND WE CAN GET BACK TO FIGHTING CRIME THE WAY IT *SHOULD* BE FOUGHT: AS A TEAM!

I'M NOT MOVING HOME.

YOU'RE NOT??

IT'S NOT JUST LARGE CITIES THAT HAVE SUPERCRIME ISSUES. THIS ONE DOES TOO.

THIS CITY *NEEDS* ME.

AAAHHGH!

THPTHP THPTHP

SEE? THE PLACE IS JUST CRAWLING WITH NINJAS.

SO GROSS! THE WAY THEY RAN BY ON THEIR TINY LITTLE FEET?? *EW.*

I'M INTERVIEWING POTENTIAL ROOM-MATES TONIGHT. WISH ME LUCK.

MAY YOU FIND A COMPLETELY NORMAL PERSON TO LIVE WITH!

HEH, I WISH.

SO, DO YOU HAVE ANY DIETARY RESTRICTIONS?

I ONLY FEAST UPON THE SOULS OF MY DEFEATED ENEMIES...

ARE YOU A LATE-NIGHT PARTIER? I HAVE TO BE AT WORK PRETTY EARLY IN THE MORNING.

SEE, I FEEL LIKE, Y'KNOW, TIME IS A TOTAL *STATE OF MIND*, MAN. AND YOU SHOULD NEVER, LIKE, LET THE FASCIST CLOCK STATE WHEN YOU KEEP YOU MAN. I DO MY DEEPEST ABOUT 3AM WHICH IS MENT WHEN THE

DO YOU HAVE ANY PETS?

MEW   MEW

...NNO.

LOOK, I JUST NEED A ROOM-MATE WHO ISN'T CRAZY AND DOESN'T KEEP ME UP AT NIGHT.

DOES THAT SOUND LIKE YOU?

OH, YES!

I'M NOT MUCH FOR PARTY-ING.

ALTH-OUGH...

UM, I DO SOMETIMES DRESS AS A SUPERHERO AND FIGHT CRIME. THAT'S NOT AN ISSUE. I HOPE

HEY, FIND A ROOMMATE?

YEP. HALF CRAZY BEATS ALL CRAZY ANY DAY.

AND SO, SUPERHERO GIRL FOUND HER PLACE IN THE WORLD.

SHE HAD A REASONABLY PRICED ROOM TO CALL HER OWN.

SHE HAD VILLAINS TO FIGHT AND A CITY TO PROTECT.

SHE WAS STILL FIGURING OUT WHO SHE WAS AND WHAT SHE WANTED IN LIFE...

...BUT THERE WAS PLENTY OF TIME FOR THAT.

SPARE CHANGE?

HEYY, I'M HOOOOME.

TOTALLY KICKED SUPERVILLAIN ASS TODAY. IT WAS GREAT.

AND THEN-- OH *CRAP!*

ZIIP

HEY, I'M...UH, HOME. FROM MY COMPLETELY NORMAL ...JOB...

OH HELLO, ROOMIE! I DID NOT KNOW YOUR BOYFRIEND WAS HERE! IT'S A GOOD THING I WAS WEARING COMPLETELY NORMAL CLOTHES!

WOW, *REALLY?*

YEP.

ACHOOO!
SNIFF. SNIFF.
COUGH HACK
SNARF SNIFF SNF

WAS THAT YOU COUGHING?

YEAH, BUT IT'S NOTHING.

YOU SOUND REALLY SICK. MAYBE YOU SHOUDN'T GO OUT.

CRIME DOESN'T TAKE A SICK DAY, SO NEITHER CAN I.

ACHOOO

SNURF

BEWARE, HUMANS! I AM THE TOY POODLE MISTRESS! GO, MY PRETTIES! SPREAD TERROR IN THE HEARTS OF MEN!

YIP YIP YIP

YIP YIP   YIP

HEY. YOU. STOP THAT.

HACHOOO

YOU'RE *SICK!* AND I BET IT'S *SUPER* CONTAGIOUS! DON'T COME NEAR ME!

JES' A SEC. *SNURF!* BLARGH.

OKAY. READY TO FIGHT.

GROSS. FLEE FROM HER GERMS, MY PRETTIES!

YIP YIP YIP

YIP YIP

KOFF KOFF HACK HURG BLEH

HEY, HOW'RE YOU FEELING?

SNORK

TERRIBLE! I DON'T HAVE *TIME* TO BE SICK.

SERIOUSLY, THIS IS TOTAL NONSENSE! SUPERHEROES DON'T GET SICK.

MAYBE IT'S YOUR BODY TELLING YOU TO TAKE A BREAK.

UGH, I JUST HOPE THERE ISN'T ANY NEW SUPERVILLAIN ACTIVITY THIS WEEK.

SNIFF

OH, SORRY, DID YOU NEED TO TELL ME SOMETHING...?

OH, NO...

I WAS JUST WAITING TO SEE IF BEING SICK MADE YOUR SUPER-POWERS GO HAYWIRE IN AN AMUSING WAY.

I'M NOT WELL ENOUGH TO GO PATROL FOR CRIME TODAY, SO YOU'LL HAVE TO DO IT.

WHAT.

JUST PUT ON MY COSTUME AND GO BEAT UP SOME EVILDOERS! IT'S NOT ROCKET SCIENCE!

BUT I CAN'T-- I DON'T HAVE SUPERPOWERS!!

MOST OF THE TIME SUPERVILLAINS RUN INSTEAD OF FIGHT. I'M SURE YOU'LL BE FINE.

UH...LOOKING GOOD AND LAW ABIDING, CITIZEN!

KEEP IT UP!

JUST... KEEPING THE PARK FREE OF CRIME.

HEH! SHE WAS RIGHT. THIS IS A PIECE OF CAKE.

GR.

KEEPIN' THE PARK FREE OF CRIME, DO DEE DOO...

AHHHHH!

BEAR BEAR BEAR BEAR WITH A MONOCLE BEEAAARR!

GRAARR

RUN LADY IT'S A BEAR!!!

RAAAAR--*

TRIP

WHAM

WHAP WHAP
WHAP WHAP
WHAP

DANG. WHY DOES THIS CITY EVEN HAVE A SUPERHERO? THESE PEOPLE DON'T NEED PROTECTING.

CLAP
CLAP Veech

SNFF

BEAR, ARE YOU CRYING?

OH, I'M SO SORRY, SUPERHERO GIRL. I DIDN'T MEAN TO CAUSE YOU PROBLEMS.

I'M NOT A REGULAR BEAR. A SCIENTIST GAVE ME SUPER-INTELLIGENCE, THEN ABANDONED ME WHEN HIS FUNDING WAS CUT. RATHER THAN WALLOW IN DESPAIR, I MADE SOMETHING OF MYSELF.

EDUCATION SEEMED THE BEST WAY TO FURTHER MY SITUATION, SO I WENT TO UNIVERSITY. GOT MY BA, THEN MY MASTERS AND DOCTORATE. NOW I'M A PROFESSOR AT CLAREMONT UNIVERSITY...AND MOST OF THE TIME I'M NO THREAT TO CIVILIZED SOCIETY...

...BUT SOMETIMES...MY BEAR INSTINCTS COME OUT, AND AWFUL THINGS HAPPEN. IT'S SO EMBARRASSING.

HEY, IT'S OKAY. WE ALL HAVE BAD DAYS.

SO...I GUESS YOU COULD SAY YOU'RE **SMARTER THAN THE AVERAGE BEAR**, HUH?

HAHAHA!

GRAARR AHHHHHH

IT'S NEW YEAR'S EVE! LET'S GO OUT!

Type Type Type

NOPE. COMPILING END-OF-THE-YEAR CRIME STATISTICS.

C'MOOON. MY BOYFRIEND'S HAVING A PARTY AND I'M GOING AND YOU SHOULD TOO!

REMEMBER WHAT HAPPENED THE *LAST* TIME I WENT TO A PARTY?

THERE WILL BE *NO* SUPERVILLAINS AT *THIS* PARTY, I PROMISE!

YOU'RE SURE?

POSITIVE.

GLAD YOU CAME! I'LL INTRODUCE YOU.

THIS IS MY ROOMMATE, SHAUN.

HI!

FLASHBACK (TO COMIC #9!!!)

YOU CAN'T BE A SUPER-HERO BECAUSE BLAH BLAH

AHHHH

HHHHGH

DUDE. WHAT DID YOU *DO*?

I...I DON'T KNOW!

HELLO AGAIN!

I AM *VERY HAPPY* SITTING *ALONE* WITH MY DRINK THANK YOU VERY MUCH.

I HAVE THIS FEELING I KNOW YOU...

WELL, YOU DON'T.

(...BECAUSE I AM HERE IN MY CIVILIAN IDENTITY. NOOOO PUNCHING PEOPLE WHEN YOU'RE IN YOUR CIVILIAN IDENTITY.)

SORRY, WHAT?

NOTHING. NOTHING AT ALL.

YOUR CIVILIAN IDENTITY--?? ARE YOU A *SUPERHERO?*

ACCORDING TO YOU, NO, I AM NOT.

LET ME GUESS WHICH SUPERHERO YOU ARE.

DUDE, I'M NOT A SUPER-HERO!

OF COURSE NOT. ARE YOU SPECTACLE?

NO!

HEY, YOU TWO ARE FINALLY TALKING! I KNEW YOU'D GET ALONG.

SHAUN IS THE BIGGEST SUPERHERO FAN *EVER*. YOU SHOULD SEE HIS ROOM. HE HAS *ALL* THE TOYS.

AND, YOU KNOW, *YOU* HAVE YOUR *EXTRA-CURRICULAR* ACTIVITIES.

WINK

DON'T FORGET TO SHOW HER YOUR ROOM, SHAUN.

THEY'RE TRYING TO SET US UP.

YEAH! WANNA SEE MY ROOM?

NO.

THIS IS MY ROOM!

KEVIN IS MY FAVOURITE SUPERHERO.

I FIGURED.

I HAVE ALL HIS MERCHANDISE. I WISH WE HAD A SUPERHERO AROUND HERE WHO WAS AS AWESOME AS HIM.

THIS IS MY LIMITED EDITION KEVIN DOLL.

WANT TO HUG HIM? HE'S VERY HUGGABLE.

YEAH, OKAY.

SQUEEZE

POP AHH

OOPS. LIMITED EDITION KEVIN!!!!

THERE YOU ARE. HOW'S IT GOING WITH SHAUN?

SHAUN IS A *JERK*. HE THINKS HE'S SOME KIND OF AUTHORITY ON SUPER-HEROES. WHAT DOES HE KNOW!

WELL, I SHOWED *HIM*. HE'LL NEVER HUG HIS STUPID LIMITED EDITION KEVIN DOLL AGAIN!

MAKE FUN OF MY SUPER-HERO ABILITIES AND YOU GET *CRUSHED*. HAHA! HE DESERVED IT. WHAT A *JERK*!

ACTUALLY...I AM STARTING TO THINK MAYBE I AM THE ONE WHO IS A JERK.

UHH...I GOTTA GO MAKE THIS RIGHT!

WHAT'S GOING ON OUT HERE?

A FLIRTATION WITH SUPERJERKDOM, FOLLOWED BY AN ATTEMPT AT REDEMPTION.

MUST BE A GOOD PARTY.

GLOOM

SHAUN?

HEH!

HEY, UM, I WAS A JERK EARLIER, AND I WANTED TO APOLOGIZE.

I BROUGHT OVER A FRIEND WHO I THINK YOU MIGHT LIKE TO MEET.

HELLO THERE! I HEARD SOMEONE MIGHT NEED CHEERING UP, SO I BROUGHT OVER A LIMITED EDITION KEVIN DOLL!

KEVIN DOLLS ARE *GUARANTEED* TO TURN A FROWN UPSIDE DOWN!

EEEEEEEE

THANKS, KEVIN.

UH... NO... PROBLEM.

POW

THIS HEAT WAVE IS THE WORST. FIGHTING CRIME IN 40 DEGREE WEATHER IS BRUTAL.

I THINK I'M LITERALLY MELTING.

YOU THINK *YOU'RE* HOT? TRY WEARING A COSTUME THAT'S HEAD-TO-TOE *BLACK*.

HMM.

WEEEEEEE PSSHH

HAHA, THAT WAS GREAT! WHAT A WAY TO BEAT THE HEAT.

YEAH!

POW